Robin Hood is probably one of the world's best-known adventure characters, and many stories about his merry band have been told since the minstrels of Old England first sang of his life. While folklorists and historians may still argue about the truth behind Robin Hood, it is clear that the notion of a playful thief with a kind heart has maintained its appeal to children and parents alike for seven centuries.

Movies, TV serials and dozens of books based on Robin Hood have been constructed atop the original few adventures, bringing with them new characters and differing historical settings that would amaze the early storytellers. Some versions have faded from sight, while others have become a permanent part of the Sherwood Forest legend.

Robin Hood was one of our favorite characters when we were kids, and before embarking on our own retelling, we pored over many versions, especially those by Paul Creswick (illustrated by N.C. Wyeth in 1917) and Howard Pyle (1884). We hope that this dog-eared condensation will entertain our young readers and inspire them to read some of the other Robin Hood tales.

John Bianchi
Frank B. Edwards

Dedicated to Buffy (1976-89)
and Molly (1984-98)

Written by John Bianchi and Frank B. Edwards
Illustrated by John Bianchi
Copyright 1999 by Pokeweed Press

Cataloguing in Publication Data

Edwards, Frank B., 1952-
    Robin Hood with lots of dogs

(Dog-eared classics series)
Illustrated condensation of two Robin Hood novels
ISBN 0-894323-09-2 (bound)   ISBN 0-921285-08-4 (pbk.)

1. Robin Hood (Legendary character) — Juvenile fiction.
I. Bianchi, John   II. Title.   III. Series.

PS8553.I26T74 1999   jC813'.54 C99-900485-6
PZ7.B47126Tr 1999

Published by:
Pokeweed Press
Suite 200
17 Elk Court
Kingston, Ontario
K7M 7A4

Visit Pokeweed Press on the Net at:
www.Pokeweed.com

Send E-mail to Pokeweed Press at:
publisher@pokeweed.com

Printed in Canada by:
Friesens Corporation

Distributed in the U.S.A. by:
General Distribution Services
Suite 202
85 River Rock Drive
Buffalo, NY   14207

Distributed in Canada by:
General Distribution Services
325 Humber College Blvd.
Toronto, ON
M9W 7C3

Visit General Distribution on the Net at:
www.genpub.com

Robin Hood

WITH LOTS OF DOGS

*A canine condensation of
Great Britain's most famous tale*

Written by
Frank B. Edwards

Illustrated by
John Bianchi

A Dog-Eared Classic

Before he grew up to become England's most famous outlaw, Robin Hood led a typical country life. He played in the woods each day with his young friends, leading them through the vast network of paths and caves of Sherwood Forest, climbing to the tops of the sprawling oak trees and swimming in the cold streams that meandered through the countryside.

But Robin Hood was no ordinary pup.

True, he was not the strongest or the biggest of the pack that played in the forest, but he was by far the most popular. His friends asked for his opinions about everything, and he became a kind and fair leader who was as wise as he was brave. Whether there was a cavern to explore or a nasty bully to confront, Robin was always the first to start any new adventure. And while his enthusiasm often earned him scrapes and bruises, he was rewarded with the love and admiration of all who knew him.

Much as he enjoyed his friends, however, his favorite companions were his bow and a quiver of arrows, for he truly wanted to become Sherwood Forest's best archer. He practiced for hours at a time, choosing targets that became smaller and more distant as he became more skilled. And each night, he dreamed of becoming a forester and gamekeeper, protecting the King's deer from poachers, while roaming freely throughout the forest.

Alas, when he grew older, Robin sadly discovered that not all dreams come true — or at least not the way we might hope.

Robin truly wanted to become Sherwood Forest's best archer.

In those ancient days, the King of England lived in London and was seldom able to visit the hundreds of villages and towns that were scattered about the land, so he appointed sheriffs in each district to oversee his subjects and enforce the laws of the land. The sheriffs lived in castles and had small armies so that they could protect the local citizens and arrest outlaws.

Many of the King's sheriffs were good, but some, like the one in Nottingham, were bad.

Unfortunately for the good folk of Sherwood Forest, the Sheriff of Nottingham was very bad, indeed. He was a cruel, evil brute who was as ruthless as he was greedy. He taxed the farmers until they had nothing left, then he took their land. He cheated the merchants and even stole some of the tax money that he was supposed to send to the King.

The Sheriff liked no one, but he particularly disliked the poor. "I work day and night to earn my riches," he often complained. "And the poor do nothing but beg me for help. Can they not learn to help each other?"

All the peasants were deathly afraid of the Sheriff, so they just accepted that life in Nottingham was unfair and hoped the Sheriff would not notice them when he was searching for his next victim.

Whenever any citizens were brave enough to set off for London to complain to the King, the Sheriff had them arrested for something they had not done and put them in his dank and dirty jail for a long time.

Or sometimes, they would just disappear altogether.

The Sheriff of Nottingham liked no one, but he particularly disliked the poor.

Each spring, every town across England held a fair to celebrate May Day. Everyone from knights and soldiers to young peasants took part in all sorts of contests to win prizes — and the applause of the crowd. There was archery, wrestling, jousting, dancing and music for the amusement of rich and poor alike.

The year he turned 15, young Robin set out for the annual celebration with a special purpose. He was finally old enough to enter the Sheriff's Golden Arrow Tournament, and Robin was determined to perform well — for the winner was often invited to become a King's forester.

Whistling merrily, he walked quickly along the wooded path, dreaming of fame and fortune, when his thoughts were interrupted by the rude laughter of a dozen local foresters who were lazing under a large oak tree.

"Where might you be going with your toy bow and tiny arrows?" barked their leader, a cruel bully who hated both whistling and smiles.

"I am off to Nottingham in search of good fortune," replied Robin. "Perhaps when the Sheriff sees my shooting, he will give me your job."

"Jobs like mine do not go to cheerful pups for merely shooting a painted target," boasted the old rogue. "You need the skill to shoot a stag at a hundred paces."

And with that, he aimed his bow at a deer drinking from a nearby stream. But quick as a flash, Robin fired an arrow of his own and felled the beast before the forester's arrow had even left his bow.

"Now what do you think of my skill?" laughed Robin.

"Methinks it has earned you a place in Nottingham Jail," howled the gamekeeper. "Grab him, you louts, and earn yourselves a rich reward."

"Perhaps when the Sheriff sees my shooting, he will give me your job," said Robin.

Poor Robin was stunned by this unexpected twist of fate and fled deep into the forest to escape. His archery skills had brought him trouble instead of fame, and the foresters were certain to tell the Sheriff of his crime. There would be no job for him at the end of this day.

As he worried about his predicament, Robin came to a rushing river that could be crossed only by walking atop a long, narrow log. He jumped onto it and was halfway over the torrent when a tall, dark hound clambered up from the other side and eased toward him.

"Make way for me, young pup," growled the stranger with a teasing smile. "And let this wild dog pass first."

"Nay, you stand back," said Robin. And with that, he lunged at the large mischief-maker, hoping to send him into the water. But, instead, his own legs were knocked out from under him, and he splashed into the river.

Paddling furiously, he made his way to shore to confront his tormentor. But the stranger was laughing so hard, he had fallen down on the bank.

"You would make a far better friend than foe," he spluttered. "You know no fear and have the spirit of a dozen pit bulls. My name is Little John, and I would be honored to call you my companion."

Robin readily accepted the offer of friendship, then explained his problem with the foresters. But Little John assured him that nothing could be done right then.

"A few coins may change their memories tomorrow," he suggested. "So let us go to the fair and see if you can win enough to buy their silence."

Robin's legs were knocked out from under him, and he splashed into the river.

When the pair arrived at the fair, the archery tournament was just over. The captain of the guard had taken his shot and was preparing to accept first prize, for he had sunk an arrow deep into the middle of the bull's-eye.

With encouragement from Little John, Robin pulled his hood up over his head so that no one would recognize him and eased his way through the crowd. Nodding to the other competitors, he sent an arrow through the shaft of the winner's, splitting it in two and replacing it in the bull's-eye.

The spectators applauded madly, for they were delighted to see the captain beaten so dramatically.

"A very fine shot by the hooded archer," announced the Sheriff, who stood holding a bag of gold and a gilded arrow for the winner. "But he arrived too late, and the prize goes to our own local champion."

Enraged by his young friend's treatment, Little John grabbed the bag of gold from the Sheriff and raced across the field toward the woods. While soldiers chased after his friend, Robin decided that it was time to depart as well. Pulling his cloak back, he jumped into a nearby viewing box and almost collided with the beautiful young maiden seated there.

"You are a fine archer but a clumsy thief," she smiled, pointing to a small exit behind her. "My name is Maid Marian. What's yours?"

"Robin Hood," he called as he tumbled out the door.

"Well, be careful, young Robin. I hope we'll meet again."

"A very fine shot by the hooded archer," announced the Sheriff.

Little John was waiting for Robin at a crossroads in Sherwood Forest that evening and greeted him with a hearty pat on the back.

"Well, here is the scoundrel known as Robin Hood, who disrupted the Sheriff's tournament this afternoon," he laughed. "You have become a valuable friend, indeed, for there is a large reward on your head."

Poor Robin felt miserable; his encounter with the deer and the Sheriff had changed his life forever. "My future is ruined," he sighed. "By morning, every soldier and forester in the county will be searching for me."

"Don't worry about your future, young pup. Sherwood offers many places to hide," soothed Little John. "Besides, you are a fine archer and a fearless fighter and much too nice a fellow to join the King's foresters. We can become thieves and prosper together without ever leaving the forest."

"But I cannot steal," said Robin. "It isn't right."

"Too late for such talk now," howled Little John. "We have the Sheriff's gold in our pockets, and you have slain one of the King's deer. Sadly, there is no justice for poor dogs like us — only bad laws and empty bowls."

"Then we shall fix that," cried Robin. "Let us become honorable thieves. We will punish the bad and reward the good. And when we find gold, we will give it to those who need it the most."

And with that declaration, the two friends swore an oath of loyalty and melted into the greenery of Sherwood Forest.

"You have become a valuable friend, indeed, for there is a large reward on your head."

Little John and Robin's career as robbers was successful from its very first day, thanks to the long, lonely road that cut through the center of Sherwood Forest. Every day, travelers journeyed through the forest on their way to and from Nottingham, and the two outlaws made it their business to stop as many of the wayfarers as possible.

Poor folk would be greeted most cheerfully and sent on their way with an extra penny or two, while farmers and merchants were usually asked to make a small donation to help the needy. Those who were generous received an invitation to Robin's hidden camp, where they feasted and sang late into the night with the outlaws. In fact, after such fine entertainment and good food, many of the victims begged to join Robin in Sherwood — for the cause was just and each day offered new adventures. By the end of that first summer, Robin had attracted 40 faithful followers.

But it did not pay to lie to Robin when he sought a donation.

"Can you spare two pieces of gold for the poor?" he would ask a well-dressed traveler riding a magnificent horse.

"Alas, but I have only five pennies," an unwilling victim would answer.

And with that, Robin would look up to the sky and beg, "St. Jude, surely you can fill this fine dog's pockets and bags with gold."

Then, before the confused noble or merchant could protest, Robin and his cohorts would ransack his luggage, pretending that each piece of hidden gold had been sent to them by magic. With a wink, Robin would thank the traveler for his honesty and give him back his five pennies.

The two outlaws made it their business to stop as many wayfarers as possible.

Few travelers knew what Robin really looked like, since his victims described him as a large and frightening mongrel rather than admit to having been robbed by a polite young pup. This allowed him to play tricks on the strangers he met who did not recognize him.

One day, a rotund friar from a nearby monastery met Robin on the bank of a stream that had neither bridge nor stepping-stones across it.

"I pray thee, good fellow," he said. "I am here in search of Robin Hood. Do you know where I might find him?"

"They say he lives on the wind and in the trees. Perhaps he is watching you right now," replied Robin, seeing a chance to play a joke on the friar. "If you carry me across the creek, perhaps we will find him there."

And so the friar allowed Robin to climb onto his back, but when they had crossed, he picked up a heavy stick and waved it at his passenger. "I see no one here," he growled. "I demand to be carried back so that my robes can dry, or I will punish you for your waggery."

Robin happily agreed and struggled mightily with his burden. But halfway across, he lost his footing and stumbled, dropping the friar into the water. The wet hound was furious and began to beat Robin, who had lunged ashore and was shaking himself dry.

"Did you seek me out so that you could beat me like a cur?" he asked.

"No," whined the friar, realizing his mistake. "If you are Robin, then I come with a message — and the hope of a taste of the King's venison."

"You shall tell us your news after we dine tonight," said Robin.

And so the friar allowed Robin to climb onto his back.

That night, Robin hosted a fine feast for Friar Tuck, who was greeted enthusiastically by the pack. After eating their fill, the outlaws staged a series of competitions to demonstrate their skill in both combat and song. The entertainment ended with a gentle ballad by Little John that told of the loneliness of life in the forest, far away from family and old friends.

"This is no time for sadness," barked Robin. "Let the good friar tell us the news from Nottingham — something that will lift our hearts."

"I bring little happy news, for Nottingham has not been a joyful place for many years," replied Friar Tuck. "I have only a private message for Robin."

"I have no secrets from my friends," declared Robin. "Tell us all."

Hesitating, his jolly guest obliged. "A fair maiden called Marian, whom you met briefly several years ago, wonders why she has heard nothing from you," said the friar. "She swears she felt the sting of Cupid's arrow in her heart that day in May and was certain that you, too, were struck. I am to arrange a meeting between you — but only if your heart is open to the sweetness that true love can bring."

At this news, Robin's companions howled with delight, as their leader seldom made his feelings known, but many had suspected that he carried a secret flame for some mysterious maiden.

"I do not remember any such damsel at the fair that day," blurted Robin, "but perhaps my memory will be refreshed after a brief visit. Tell her to meet me at the Blue Boar Inn three days hence."

Robin's companions howled with delight.

The Blue Boar Inn was a day's journey from the outlaw camp, and Robin arrived there in early evening, dressed as a ragged peddler. Although the food and drink were good, it was a dangerous place for outlaws and travelers alike. Travelers on the road to Nottingham had much to fear from loitering robbers, and careless outlaws were easy prey for passing soldiers or the Sheriff's spies.

And so it was that Robin sat disguised at a table outside, underneath an old oak, ready to flee from danger but also in search of Maid Marian, the short-eared beauty who had caught his eye and captured his heart so long ago.

But, instead, a nervous young page sat down beside him.

"Rest easy, young pup," said Robin. "Have you come far?"

"From Nottingham. I am here to meet a friend, but I fear he has not come, and my trip was in vain."

"This is an odd spot to meet a friend," Robin observed.

"Nottingham is too dangerous a place for him," the page explained.

"Surely that is true for everyone, though," said Robin.

"Alas, the Sheriff steals from us all equally, making our lives more miserable each day, because he rules by greed instead of by law. But his hatred of my friend is such that I pray for his life each night."

"I know your friend well, Marian," whispered Robin as he patted the disguised page's shoulder. "And he thinks of you each day too."

"I know your friend well, Marian," whispered Robin. "He thinks of you each day."

Maid Marian was greatly relieved to hear of Robin's love, and the two promised that they would marry when Robin's freedom was no longer threatened. They talked long into the night. Robin told of his adventures in Sherwood, but Maid Marian spoke of the Sheriff's tyranny in Nottingham. Her parents and many of their neighbors had lost their land to his greed, and each year, taxes rose and punishments became harsher.

"That scoundrel must be taught a lesson," growled Robin.

The next day, Robin set off for Nottingham, stopping along the way to visit a butcher who sold him his meat, his cart and his apron for a fair price. Disguised as a vendor, Robin set up a stall in the market and caused a sensation by selling meat at such low prices that everything was gone by noon. The other merchants assumed he was mad, for no one could understand how the new butcher would stay in business.

"I must confess," Robin told his neighbors, "that I do not like this butchery business. My father's cattle fell into my hands after his death, but I would rather give them away than have to slaughter another one."

When word reached the Sheriff that there was a bargain to be had, he rushed to the market and introduced himself to the mad butcher.

"I like cattle and would buy your herd for a good price," he said.

"I love them as brothers," said Robin, "but I would sell all 200 for 100 pieces of gold."

It was a bargain, indeed, and the Sheriff invited Robin to spend the night at his castle so that they could inspect the herd early the next morning. Robin agreed but begged for a simple bed on the kitchen floor.

The Sheriff rushed to the market and introduced himself to the mad butcher.

As soon as the Sheriff and his servants were asleep, Robin prowled through the kitchen and took his host's finest wines and a large assortment of gold and silver plates, goblets and cutlery. By dawn, he had hidden everything in his butcher's cart and was ready for the trip to view his cattle.

The Sheriff awoke in an excellent mood and thoroughly enjoyed the first part of the journey, listening to the simple butcher prattle on mindlessly about the joys of a country life. But his pleasure changed to caution as Robin steered his cart onto the road that entered Sherwood Forest.

"Where are we going, you fool?" he snarled. "There are no farms here."

"Ah, but my herd is in a clearing nearby," explained Robin, and they continued for another mile, while the Sheriff became more nervous.

Finally, they rounded a bend and came upon a herd of the King's deer.

"There they are. Fit for a king," laughed Robin, as he blew his horn.

They were quickly surrounded by his companions, including Little John, who wanted to hang the Sheriff from the nearest tree.

"That is not how we treat our richest guests," growled Robin. "Tell Friar Tuck to prepare a feast while I arrange payment for my antlered cattle."

The Sheriff was furious when Robin relieved him of his gold, but when he sat down to dine, he became even more outraged, for the feast was set out on his finest plates, and the goblets were filled with his best wines.

When at last the meal was over, Little John tied the Sheriff onto a donkey and fixed antlers to his head before sending the rogue back to town.

Little John tied the Sheriff onto a donkey and fixed antlers to his head.

The Sheriff was furious about Robin's trick. Not only had he lost some of his precious gold, but the story of his foolish return to Nottingham had spread rapidly. Whenever he walked through the streets, he was sure he heard the townsfolk making low mooing sounds.

"I will have my revenge on that outlaw if I have to cut down every tree in Sherwood Forest to find him," he vowed. And with that promise, he began to craft a devious plan.

First, he gathered all his soldiers and arrested Maid Marian (for she had told too many of her neighbors about her love for Robin). Then he placed her upon a horse and led his army and hostage along the road into Sherwood Forest, scattering all travelers out of his way.

He had just knocked a group of cloaked monks into the bushes when he halted and howled to the trees, "Robin Hood, I have heard stories of your interest in this lovely young damsel. Please come and pay your respects."

Robin, who had observed the procession's approach, swooped down from a large tree and snatched Maid Marian from her captors while his merry band fearlessly attacked the soldiers. But the battle lasted for only a few minutes, because Robin's friends were hopelessly outnumbered.

The soldiers seized Robin and struggled to drop a noose around his neck. They planned to hang him from a nearby oak.

Pointing to the poor monks who had witnessed the drama, the Sheriff snarled at the abbot who led them, "Prepare a suitable blessing for this condemned outlaw, and be quick about it."

Robin's friends were hopelessly outnumbered.

"Alas, we cannot offer up any such blessing," said the abbot, stepping forward, "for we are only poor soldiers returning from the wars. We were told to disguise ourselves because of the danger from outlaws, but it seems there is far more to fear from the Sheriff."

"You insolent dog," foamed the Sheriff. "You will hang beside this thief for your impertinence." And he ordered his soldiers to seize the masquerading monks as well.

But in the struggle, the abbot's cloak fell to the ground, revealing a battle tunic emblazoned with the King's coat of arms.

Robin fell to his knees. "King Richard, welcome to Sherwood Forest."

The Sheriff was speechless and slid from his horse to bow before the monarch, but the King dismissed him with a wave of his paw. "Begone, you villain. Go back to Nottingham, and prepare for your King's arrival. I am touring the land to see what has become of my subjects. You have shown me much already today."

As the Sheriff and his soldiers quickly departed, the King freed Robin Hood from his bonds and gazed fondly at him and Maid Marian.

"In truth, Robin, I have heard many stories about your kindness, and I traveled this way to visit you," he said. "It seems that many things have gone wrong across my kingdom, and I came to deliver justice — but not with a scaffold."

And with that, he pulled out his sword and tapped the kneeling Robin lightly on the shoulder, saying, "Arise, Sir Robin, Protector of the Poor."

"Arise, Sir Robin, Protector of the Poor."

Maid Marian rushed to Robin, who said, "Your Majesty, will you join my future bride and me at a feast to celebrate your return and my good fortune?"

And they headed to Robin's camp, where Friar Tuck organized a meal like no other before. After an evening of food, song and displays of archery and wrestling, the celebrants fell asleep where they sat.

The next morning, King Richard announced that he would make Robin the new Sheriff of Nottingham, but Robin declined.

"I love the great outdoors and adventure too much, my lord," he said. "I beg you to find someone better suited for a life in town."

And the King agreed. Instead, he invited Robin and his band to join him on his tour of the kingdom. Their loyalty and skill as archers won them a place in the King's heart, and they stayed with him as soldiers and bodyguards.

But Robin's love of Sherwood Forest was almost as great as his love for Maid Marian, so the two were married and eventually returned to Sherwood, where they kept an estate and raised a family. Peace had settled over the land, and their pups roamed freely and happily amid the streams and trails that their father had followed so many years before.